Wake Up, Mummy!

KT-527-182

igloobooks

Wake up, Mummy!
Get out of bed.
It's time to get up
now, sleepyhead.

I'm wide awake. Teddy Bear is, too.
We're excited for the day. Why aren't you?

This igloo book belongs to:

....

igloobooks

Published in 2020
by Igloo Books Ltd, Cottage Farm, Sywell, NN6 0BJ
www.igloobooks.com

Copyright © 2017 Igloo Books Ltd
Igloo Books is an imprint of Bonnier Books UK

All rights reserved. No part of this publication may be
reproduced or transmitted in any form or by any means,
electronic, or mechanical, including photocopying, recording,
or by any information storage and retrieval system,
without permission in writing from the publisher.

Written by Stephanie Moss
Illustrated by Steve Brown

Cover designed by Justine Ablett & Nicholas Gage
Interiors designed by Justine Ablett
Edited by Stephanie Moss

0220 004
6 8 10 12 11 9 7 5
ISBN 978-1-78670-141-1

Printed and manufactured in China

Wake up, Mummy!
Let's start the morning.
Don't try and hide.
I can see you yawning.
You can wriggle away
under your cosy sheet,
but if you don't get up
soon, I'll **stamp** my feet!

What's that sound?
Is it a **TWIT-TWOO?**

Listen! The whole world
is awake, except you.

Wake up, Mummy! Let's pick out your clothes.
A dressing gown will do for now, I suppose.

Here's one slipper, the other's somewhere about. Oh, no! Your dressing gown's on inside out!

Wake up, Mummy!
I'm ready to play.
You still look awfully
sleepy, I must say.

I can't wait to have fun with all of my toys.
If you're not awake soon, I'll make even more **noise!**

Wake up, Mummy! Come with me.
All you need is a nice cup of tea.

Let's make pancakes as a
special surprise.
I'll share them with Daddy,
when he opens his eyes.

Wake up, Mummy! I love to hear the birds sing.
Oh, for some reason, I can't hear anything.

I'm going to play with the dog. Come here, good boy!
You normally love fetching your fluffy rope-toy?

Wake up, Mummy! I want a milky drink.
Morning is the best time of day, don't you think?

Mummy, you're
spilling the milk.

No... wait...

STOP!

I'll go and brush my teeth,
while you get the mop.

Wake up, Mummy! Hang on, why isn't it light?
It looks like it's still the middle of the night!

It's a lot darker than normal,
or is it just me?

Maybe we **are** up
earlier than we'd
usually be.

Wake up, Mummy!
Well, if you must have a snooze,
a quick little nap isn't too
much time to lose.

Let's get back into bed for
just a minute or two.
The new day can wait while
I cuddle up with you.